Nat the Cat
Has a Hat

By Jarrett Lerner

Ready-to-Read

Simon Spotlight

New York   Amsterdam/Antwerp   London   Toronto   Sydney   New Delhi

For Paul and the whole Silver Unicorn Bookstore crew

SIMON SPOTLIGHT
An imprint of Simon & Schuster Children's Publishing Division
1230 Avenue of the Americas, New York, New York 10020
This Simon Spotlight edition January 2025
Copyright © 2025 by Jarrett Lerner
All rights reserved, including the right of reproduction
in whole or in part in any form.
SIMON SPOTLIGHT, READY-TO-READ, and colophon
are registered trademarks of Simon & Schuster, LLC.
For information about special discounts for bulk purchases,
please contact Simon & Schuster Special Sales at 1-866-506-1949
or business@simonandschuster.com.
Manufactured in the United States of America 1124 LAK
2 4 6 8 10 9 7 5 3 1
This book has been cataloged with the Library of Congress.
ISBN 978-1-6659-5712-0 (hc)
ISBN 978-1-6659-5711-3 (pbk)
ISBN 978-1-6659-5713-7 (ebook)

This is Nat.

Nat is a cat.

It is
a nice hat,
Nat.

This is Pat.

Pat is a rat.

Pat the Rat also has a hat!

Does Nat the Cat
want a hat
like that?

One new hat
for Nat the Cat!

Does Nat the Cat
want a hat
like THAT?

NOD! NOD! NOD! NOD!

Here you go,
Nat.

What is wrong, Nat?

This is getting very,
very, very SILLY,
Nat the Cat.

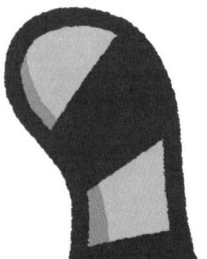

Or maybe . . .